Little Red Robin

The Fleas Who Fight Crime

Do you have all the Little Red Robin books?

- [ ] Buster's Big Surprise
- [ ] The Purple Butterfly
- [ ] How Bobby Got His Pet
- [ ] We are Super!
- [ ] New Friends
- [ ] Robo-Robbie
- [ ] The Fleas Who Fight Crime
- [ ] A Friend for Dragon
- [ ] When the Tooth Fairy Forgot
- [ ] Silly Name for a Monster

Also available as ebooks

If you feel ready to read a longer book, look out for more stories about Buzz and Itch

Little Red
Robin

Jonny Zucker
Illustrated by Chris Jevons

SCHOLASTIC

Scholastic Children's Books
An imprint of Scholastic Ltd.
Euston House, 24 Eversholt Street
London, NW1 1DB, UK
Registered office: Westfield Road, Southam, Warwickshire, CV47 0RA

First published in the UK in 2014 by Scholastic Ltd

ISBN 978 1407 14294 4

A CIP catalogue record for this book is available from the British Library

Printed in China.

1 3 5 7 9 10 8 6 4 2

www.scholastic.co.uk

Buzz and Itch were fleas.

Buzz lived to the north of Larva Town.

Itch lived to the south of Larva Town.

Itch wanted to be an insect detective and nab insect villains.

Buzz wanted to be an insect detective and catch insect criminals.

Buzz's favourite magazine was *Insect Crime Monthly*.

Itch's favourite magazine was *Insect Crime Monthly*.

Insect Crime Monthly was all about the crimes that happened in Larva Town.

If I want to catch insect criminals, I need to head to Larva Town!
thought Buzz.

If I want to nab insect villains – and get my picture in Insect Crime Monthly *– I need to make flea tracks to Larva Town!*
thought Itch.

So Buzz set off
towards Larva Town
from the north.

And Itch set off
for Larva Town
from the south.

Buzz ate his dung sandwich halfway through the journey.

Itch ate *his* dung sandwich five minutes after he set out.

It was night by the time the two fleas reached Larva Town.

Buzz saw glow-worms lighting up the streets and shops.

Itch heard the hum of laughter and the chatter of insects.

"Wow, this looks great!" murmured Buzz.

"Wow, this place is awesome!" murmured Itch.

West Side
Honey Store
Official
Beetles
Record
Store
Maggot
Supermarket
Insect
Shoes
Ant
Playgroup

The two fleas bumped into each other at the edge of the West Side Wood.

"Who are you?" demanded Itch.

"I'm Buzz," said Buzz, "and I'm going to be Larva Town's chief insect-criminal catcher!"

"Well I'm Itch," said Itch, "and *I'm* going to be Larva Town's chief insect-villain nabber!"

"Can you keep the noise down?" asked a sleepy white rabbit, opening one eye. She was lying in a hutch at the end of a human family's garden.

"What a stroke of luck," smiled Buzz. "Could I possibly live in your fur for a few days?"

"My name's Lambert," yawned the rabbit. "If you're quiet and you let me sleep, you can *both* live in my fur."

"Thanks!" shouted Buzz, running up Lambert's back and pulling some of her fur over himself as a blanket.

"Hey, that's where *I* wanted to sleep!" cried Itch, sprinting up Lambert's back and pushing Buzz out of the way.

"Boys!" scolded Lambert.

The next morning when Buzz and Itch woke up, an anxious-looking ladybird flew into view. "All of the sweets from my Sweet Grotto at the Larva Town Carnival have been stolen!" groaned the ladybird. "They're worth hundreds of Bug Notes and the town's kids are going crazy without my sweets."

"I'm going to the carnival to catch the sweet-stealer myself!" declared Buzz.

"I bet I nab the crook before you!" said Itch.

Itch started shaking his abdomen and kicking his legs out, until his whole body was a blur.

"Er . . . what are you doing?" demanded Buzz.

"I'm trying to fly," replied Itch.

"We're fleas!" said Buzz,
yanking Itch to a stop.
"We don't fly, we jump!"

Itch glared at Buzz.

When Buzz
took one path
to the carnival,
Itch took another.

The carnival was being held in Larva Town Square.

There were colourful floats, balloons and flags wherever you looked.

Buzz went straight to the Fleacups Ride. A bee in one of the fleacups had suspicious-looking eyes, but when Buzz checked inside her fleacup, there were no sweets to be found.

Itch went straight to the Throw a Hoop into the Spider's Mouth stall. The spider had a shifty-looking extra-hairy beard, but when Itch looked in the spider's open mouth, he couldn't see even one sweet.

Box o'
Hoops

Next Buzz went to the Gnat World of Mirrors and Itch visited the Midge Wrestling Tent. There were no stolen sweets in either.

A few minutes later, Buzz and Itch arrived at the Dragonfly Ghost House at the same time. The ghost house was run by a dragonfly with white specks on his wings.

"That'll be two Bug Notes each," said the dragonfly.

"I'm going in first," said Buzz, handing over two Bug Notes.

"No, I am!" said Itch, chucking his Bug Notes at the dragonfly and racing inside.

The Dragonfly Ghost House was pretty dark inside and dirty, with lots of pieces of paper on the ground. But it wasn't scary. A cardboard "Dragonfly of Doom" appeared and made a feeble roaring noise, while a tiny green mud "Monster Dragonfly" trilled that it would eat you.

"That was rubbish," said Itch when they emerged back into the sunlight.

"I *have* to crack this case," said Buzz, hurrying off to the Ant Trampolining Centre.

He checked out all of the ants' nettle trampolines. He looked under them, he looked over them, he looked inside them, but there were no sweets hidden anywhere.

Itch headed for the Pin The Stripe On The Bee stall.

He touched the sticky bee stripes, he smelled them, he even tasted them (they were disgusting) but all of the stripes were sweet-free.

It was getting late when a disappointed Buzz and a dejected Itch found themselves sitting at opposite ends of a twig bench.

"I guess we're no good at being insect criminal catchers," said Buzz sadly.

At that moment, they saw the dragonfly from the Dragonfly Ghost House pushing a trolley down the path. In the trolley was a big purple sack.

"What have you got in there?" called out Itch.

"Just the Bug Notes I earned today," replied the dragonfly, but as he passed by, the sack caught on a branch and split open. Sweets spilled out everywhere!

"THE DRAGONFLY IS THE SWEET THIEF!" shouted Buzz and Itch at exactly the same time.

"Those white dots on the dragonfly's wings must be tiny bits of sugar from all of the stolen sweets!" cried Buzz.

"And those pieces of paper on the floor of the Dragonfly Ghost House must be discarded wrappers from the stolen sweets!" shouted Itch.

They leaped off the bench and raced after the dragonfly.

The dragonfly started beating his wings and in a few moments he began to fly away.

"HE'S TOO FAST FOR US!" panted Itch. "WE'LL NEVER CATCH HIM!"

"FOLLOW ME!" cried Buzz, racing towards the Ant Trampoling Centre.

"Er . . . this is no time for fun!" protested Itch.

"JUST JUMP!" commanded Buzz.

Itch and Buzz jumped forward and landed on a large green nettle trampoline. They bounced off it and went hurtling into the air.

As they began to fall back down to earth, Buzz locked his antenna with Itch's.

The dragonfly was flying forward when something from the sky came crashing down towards him.

"HELP!" shrieked the dragonfly. But he was too late.

The tied-together fleas were big enough and heavy enough to knock the dragonfly to the ground with a loud THUD.

Buzz and Itch sat on the dragonfly's back and stopped him from moving.

"GOT YOU!" said a brown cockroach with a gleaming white letter "S" on his back.

"Who are you?" asked Buzz.

"I'm Sheriff Blatt, the town's law enforcer," replied the cockroach as he put the dragonfly in handcuffs.

"We found the clues, we bounced off that trampoline, we nabbed the villain!" exclaimed Itch angrily.

"Thanks for your help," replied the sheriff, steering the dragonfly off towards Larva Town's jail.

As Buzz and Itch untangled their antennae, the ladybird appeared.

"How can I ever thank you?" she asked with an enormous grin on her face.

"How about a million Bug Notes?" asked Itch hopefully as Buzz replied modestly, "There's no charge for catching fiends."

The ladybird hugged them and hurried back to her stall, with loads of insect children cheering and running behind her.

"I knew I could nail criminals!" cried Itch delightedly.

"*We* caught that dragonfly," pointed out Buzz, "by working as a *team*!"

"Really?" asked Itch. "I thought I did it by myself."

"No," said Buzz, "it was a *joint* effort!"

"You might be right," nodded Itch.

"Hey!" said Buzz. "Why don't we work TOGETHER? That way we could catch more criminals and villains!"

"Interesting idea," said Itch. "We could be called *Itch's Villain-Nabbing Organization*!"

"How about *The Fleatectives Crime-Crushing Agency*!" cried Buzz.

"That's exactly what I was going to say!" said Itch. "Can my photo be much bigger on the front page of our brochure?"

"Yes," nodded Buzz, "so long as my photo is in there *somewhere*!"

"That's settled then," beamed Itch, "we're a TEAM!"

Instead of glaring at each other, Buzz and Itch bumped thoraxes.

Then Itch started stamping his legs on the ground and wiggling his antennae from side to side.

"Er . . . Itch, what are you doing?" asked Buzz.

"I'm trying to fly," shouted Itch.

"We can't fly!" said Buzz. "We're fleas! We jump!"

Itch sighed but quickly brightened up. "Well, let's see who can jump the highest," he said.

"You're on!" laughed Buzz.

And with that, the two Fleatectives set off towards the dazzling orange sunset, bouncing up and down and talking about all of the insect villains they would soon be catching *together*.